A Tale
from
Paleface Creek

ROBERT F. MORNEAU

ILLUSTRATIONS BY MARJORIE THYSSEN MAU

PAULIST PRESS
New York / Mahwah, N.J.

Caseside illustration by Marjorie Thyssen Mau
Caseside design by Therese J. Borchard

Library of Congress Cataloging-in-Publication Data

Morneau, Robert F., 1938-
 A tale from Paleface Creek / Robert F. Morneau ; illustrations by Marjorie Thyssen Mau.
  p. cm.
 Summary: Barry the beaver, who works constantly, discovers from his animal friends that his life is more balanced if he sets time aside for such things as prayer, leisure, and love.
 ISBN: 0-8091-6678-X
  [1. Conduct of life—Fiction. 2. Beavers—Fiction. 3. Animals—Fiction.] I. Mau, Marjorie, ill. II. Title.

PZ7.M826915 Tal 2000
[Fic]—dc21
                                                                    00-057455

Published by Paulist Press
997 Macarthur Boulevard
Mahwah, New Jersey 07430

www.paulistpress.com

Printed and bound in Mexico.

Dedicated to my great grandnephew and nieces:
Charlie, Brigid, Lauren, Alexis, and Gwen.
May you have a love for all of God's creation.
—R. F. M.

To my grandsons: Nicholas, Zachary, Samuel, and Sidney.
May you always know the way of the beaver.
—M. T. M.

A thank you to the Bishop family of Paleface Creek
in Northern Michigan, who welcomed me
to observe the beaver life there in all seasons.

Barry was a busy beaver. He worked and worked and worked, from dusk to dawn, from supper to midnight, and sometimes past sunrise.

Barry could hear the voices of his father and of his grandpa ringing in his ears: *"Work! Work! Work!"*

As you can see, the family's *vocabulary* was very limited.

Barry's whole life involved building dams, one after another. The first dam he built was on the Black River, just north of Rainbow Falls, and a fine structure it was.

It provided housing for his beautiful wife, Beulah, and their eight handsome children.

Then Barry began a new dam on Paleface Creek, a creek nestled between two slopes of a deep ravine.

The work began late Monday evening, and by Friday morning Barry had a marvelous dam almost finished.

That weekend some strange things began to happen along the banks of Paleface Creek.

It was Sunday morning. Barry, with teeth well sharpened, was chomping away on a young yellow birch tree. The chips were flying, and Barry was muttering like his grandpa used to mutter:

"When a job is once begun,
never leave until it's done.
Be the job big or small,
do it well or not at all."

While muttering, Barry heard a tiny, distant sound that sang and sang and sang as it moved through the forest.

Barry listened carefully but could not figure out just what the sound was. He was pondering what he heard when his friend Cormac the crow flew overhead.

Barry shouted: "Cormac, could you come here for a minute? I have an important question to ask you."

"Mornin'," Cormac squawked.

"Mornin', Cormac," Barry replied. "Can you help me? What is that sound I hear singing through the woods?"

Cormac listened intently and then responded: "Those are bells you hear for people goin' to church. The bells are inviting them to *prayer*. You know, Barry, there's somethin' more to life than just work, work, work. There's time set aside to give thanks for all the gifts of life."

That day Barry added a new word to his vocabulary: *prayer!* Every Sunday, when the sound sang through the woods, that word *prayer* came back to mind.

Work on the lodge in the
stream bank was going well.
By midweek, however,
something happened in
Barry's life that made him
pause again and think
some more. Oscar the owl
had perched himself atop
the creek sign while Barry
was lugging a large log down
the south slope bordering Paleface
Creek.

Oscar, like most owls, was a wise fellow. He
would sit in maple trees and on fence posts and
atop towering pines hour after hour, thinking
about life and all its lessons.

PALEFACE CREE

Oscar knew all of Barry's hardworking relatives, and he had one great wish: to enlarge their vocabularies. In fact, Oscar wanted to enlarge the vocabularies of all the beavers who lived along Paleface Creek. He wanted the beavers to know that there were words other than *work* and that life held more than work.

"B-a-r-r-y," Oscar hooted, "just to the south of here there's a beautiful stand of tall hemlocks. Yesterday someone tied a hammock between two of them. Why not take a break and enjoy some *leisure*?"

Barry paused for a moment and wondered what *leisure* was. It was a funny-sounding word. As for hammock, he had never seen or heard of such a thing.

"Thanks, Oscar, for the free advice," said Barry, "but I'm busy as a bee building this beautiful lodge. Winter's coming, you know. And I have work, work, work to do."

Still, as he worked, Barry could not help thinking about the new words that had settled in his mind: *prayer* and *leisure*.

Barry caught himself muttering again: "Too many words in a beaver's head: a dangerous thing, a thing to dread."

Later that week, the first flakes of winter began to fall. Barry was so busy adding food to the winter supply that he hardly noticed the snow. One evening after supper, Beulah told Barry that she had had a visitor.

"Our good otter friend, Olivia, stopped by for tea and twigs," Beulah said. "She expressed concern for you, for me, and our children."

Barry's wife continued, "We talked about how all you do is work, work, work. You know, all work and no play makes beavers and otters and owls and crows ugly little fellows. That leaves you no time off to show us your love or to talk to me very much."

Well, you can imagine how Barry felt! He always believed he was the best of fathers and the most considerate of husbands. By working all the time he thought he provided for all of his family's needs, with a place to live and food to eat for winter.

Barry was down in the dumps in his new dam. The muttering began again. And much to his surprise, this is what came out:

"When the truth a friend does tell, good luck is near, so heed it well."

Barry spotted Millie swimming playfully upstream in Paleface Creek. "Millie," Barry called out, "I'm down in the dumps and can't find a way out. All I do is work and work and work. My vocabulary is so small I don't know what else to do but work."

Millie danced laughingly in the water and told Barry that she would tell him a great secret. But there was one condition: Barry had to promise to listen to her carefully and then practice the secret every day.

Then Millie whispered this one word into Barry's ear:

"Enough!"

Barry was really confused. "Enough? What does that mean? Enough what?"

Millie said: "It's a new word for your vocabulary. Enough is enough. Too much is too much. By that I mean enough work is enough work. There's more to life than work."

From that moment on, Barry lived the secret that Millie taught him. He limited his work to ten hours every night. And what a surprise! He still had time to hear the bells and pray, to swing in the hammock and relax, to picnic with his wife, Beulah, and their happy children.

Someday you might find yourself hiking down to Paleface
Creek. You may even hear the echo of a beaver's cheerful
mutter:
"A little work, a little play,
a little love—all this I pray,
will make my life a pleasant thing:
This is now the song I sing."